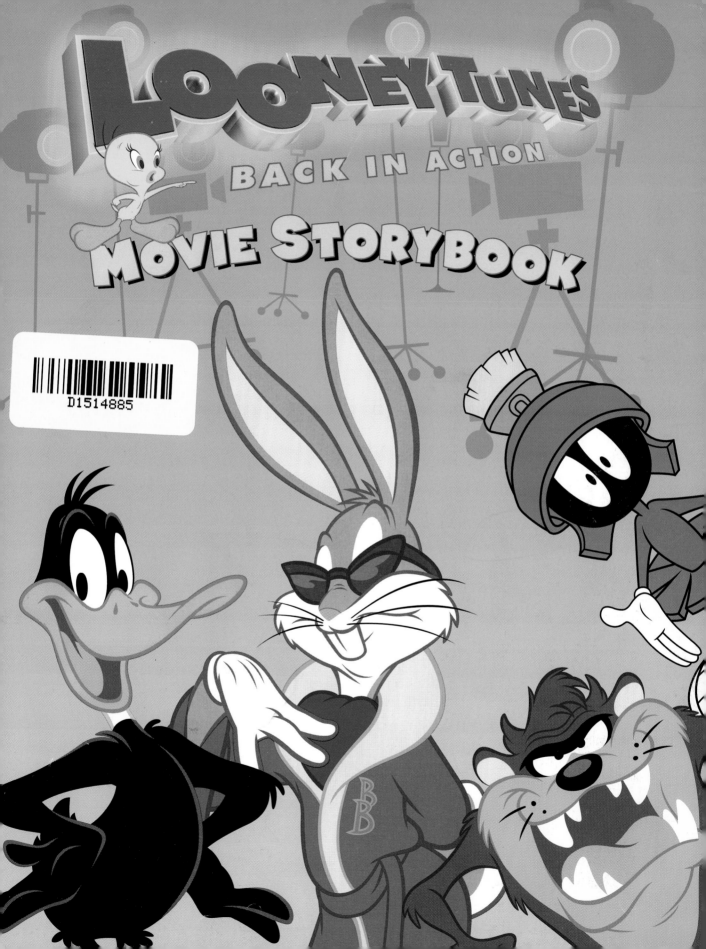

Looney Tunes
BACK IN ACTION
Movie Storybook

D1514885

DON'T MISS THESE OTHER LOONEY TUNES BACK IN ACTION BOOKS FROM SCHOLASTIC:

Looney Tunes
Back in Action
Junior Novelization
Adapted by Jenny Markas

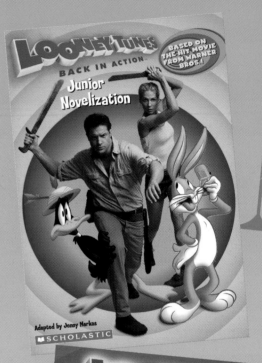

Looney Tunes
Back in Action
Joke Book
By Jesse Leon McCann

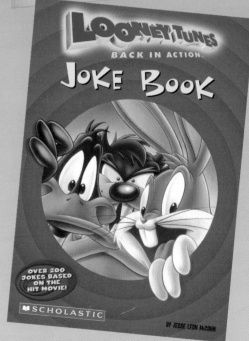

Looney Tunes
BACK IN ACTION™
MOVIE STORYBOOK

SCHOLASTIC INC.

New York   Toronto   London   Auckland   Sydney
Mexico City   New Delhi   Hong Kong   Buenos Aires

ISBN 0-439-52137-8

12 11 10 9 8 7 6 5 4 3 2 1   3 4 5 6 7 8/0
Printed in the U.S.A.
First printing, October 2003

Daffy Duck and Bugs Bunny stood before the barrel of Elmer Fudd's shotgun.

"Hey, what's up, Doc?" Bugs asked Elmer.

"I'll tell you what's up," Elmer said, nodding wisely. "It's wabbit hunting season!"

Bugs chomped on his carrot. "No, Doc. This ain't rabbit hunting season, it's duck hunting season."

Daffy shook his head angrily. "No it's not! It's wabbit season!"

"Duck season," Bugs insisted.

"Wabbit season," Daffy cried.

"Duck season!" Bugs said.

"Wabbit season!" Daffy said.

"Wabbit season!" Bugs agreed.

"Duck season, and I say fire!" Daffy cried.

Elmer promptly shot him in the head. Daffy's bill spun around backward. He'd been tricked! "Let's try that again . . ." he muttered. "No wait, I've had enough of this! I can't take it anymore!"

The lights went up in a Hollywood conference room. Daffy Duck sat at a long table with the Warner Brothers. They were watching scenes from the new Looney Tunes movie.

"I've had enough," Daffy declared. "I'm tired of playing second banana to that despicable rabbit! Either he goes or I go!"

At that moment, Bugs Bunny sauntered into the room. He was followed by several assistants. "Eh, what's up, Doc?"

"Well, you can't have a Bugs Bunny movie without Bugs Bunny," said a young woman entering behind Bugs. "Kate Houghton," she introduced herself to Daffy.

Daffy's head began to shrink like a balloon that was losing air. But he wasn't going to give up!

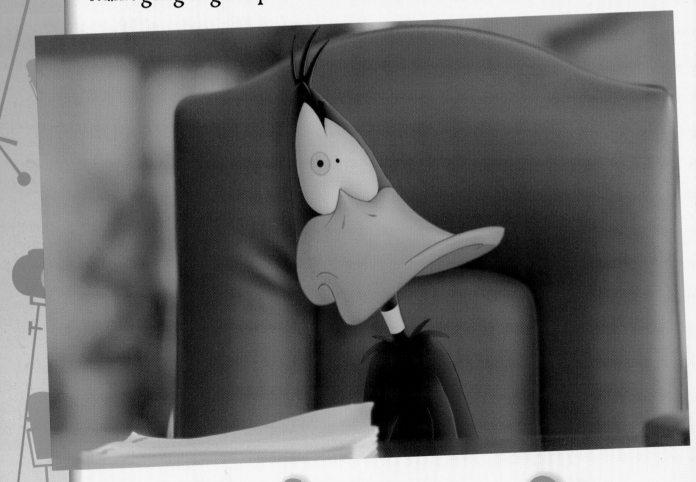

"Today's moviegoers demand action heroes! Like me!" Daffy declared.
He performed a quick series of martial arts moves, getting his arm stuck
through his head in the process.

"Top that, Rabbit!" he challenged.

Bugs struck a karate pose and flicked the back of Daffy's head. Daffy's eyes popped out and bounced along the table.

Blinded, Daffy swung his arms wildly, trying to get his eyes back. "Despicable," he muttered. Finally, he caught them and popped them back in. "I'm afraid you must choose between Bugs Bunny and me," he said.

The Warner Brothers looked at Kate. "Fire Daffy Duck," they said together.

Kate led Daffy out of the building to the studio lot.

"I need you to eject this duck," she told a security guard named DJ.

The security guard looked surprised. "This is Daffy Duck," he protested.

Daffy didn't stick around to listen to them argue. He escaped into a movie set, dodging stagehands carrying scenery and props.

DJ chased the dastardly duck past a performing elephant, into a giant crane, up the hanging scenery, and onto the ledge of a huge Gothic building.

Just below, Daffy hopped into the Batmobile. "To the duckcave!" he cried.

Only Daffy wasn't going anywhere, because DJ had him by the throat.

DJ carried the defeated Daffy back to Kate. He didn't see the flames shoot out of the back of the Batmobile. The car took off, racing across the studio. A second later, it crashed into the Warner Brothers' water tower.

Just as DJ got to Kate, the studio lot was pummeled by a giant wave of water. Practically the entire studio was destroyed.

The broken water tower caused so much damage that DJ was fired on the spot. He headed home, feeling frustrated. Even the sight of Granny, Tweety, and the prowling Sylvester next door didn't cheer him up. It wasn't his fault the studio was flooded!

To make matters worse, Daffy wouldn't leave him alone. As soon as he walked in the house, the crazy duck popped out of his gym bag!

"Get out of my father's house," DJ said.

Daffy glanced at the movie posters on the walls. His eyes bugged out. "Your dad's Damian Drake, the superspy?"

"He's an actor who *plays* a spy in the movies," DJ corrected.

Just then the TV remote control started to ring. Confused, DJ picked it up and pushed a button. A painting scrolled up, revealing a plain canvas screen. Then an old radio projected an image onto it: DJ's dad.

DJ blinked in surprise. "Dad, why are you in the painting?"

"Listen, son," he said. "I love you. I wanted to leave you out of this, but there's no one else I can trust."

Damian Drake's face disappeared and a thug appeared in its place. Then Damian's fist slammed into the thug, knocking him over.

"Dad, are you shooting a movie or something?" DJ asked. He was starting to worry.

"Come to Las Vegas," Damian said, back on the screen. "Ask Dusty Tails about the Blue Monkey – it's a diamond."

DJ tried to remain calm. "Should I call the police?"

"No. I'm sorry I didn't tell you this before, but –"

There was a scuffle, and the image on the canvas became a dark blur. Then DJ's dad was gone.

Daffy's eyes were as wide as saucers. "A diamond!" he chortled. "I'm rich!"

DJ ignored him and strode toward the door. "I've gotta go save my dad."

Daffy followed DJ out of the house. "Spies and diamonds!" he said excitedly. "This is a job for Duck. Daff Duck! Are we taking a spy car?"

"No." DJ headed toward the garage. Once inside, he climbed into his dad's old Gremlin. Daffy popped up in the passenger seat, but DJ tossed him out the window. By the time he had pulled out of the garage, Daffy had popped back in. He was excited. So excited that he called Bugs Bunny to brag.

"You can keep your Looney movie," he said. "I'm on my way to Vegas to score the Blue Monkey, a huge diamond!"

As the Gremlin sped away, the garage floor flipped over, revealing a supersleek spy car.

Meanwhile, at ACME headquarters, a sinister-looking Chairman sat at a conference table with an assistant named Mr. Smith and several other men.

"Bad news, my friends," the Chairman said. "Damian Drake's son knows about the Blue Monkey and is on his way to Las Vegas. He must not learn the location of the diamond before we do. We must get that diamond and use it for our own evil purposes!"

11

At the same time, back at the Warner Brothers' studio, Kate and Bugs Bunny were trying to make a Looney Tunes movie without Daffy Duck. It wasn't easy. Whenever Bugs Bunny or Elmer Fudd whacked a fake Daffy over the head, the fake Daffy fell down and didn't get up.

Over lunch at the studio commissary, Kate, the Warner Brothers, and Bugs sat down to discuss the issue. "Let's see," said Bugs. "We need a duck who can take a blast to the head and still keep going. Who could it be?"

Mr. Warner turned to Kate. "You're fired," he said casually.

"You got rid of our best duck," Mr. Warner's brother added.

Kate looked determined. "I'll have the real Daffy back by Monday," she said.

Later that afternoon, Kate climbed out of a cab at DJ's house. She searched the place, but DJ and Daffy were nowhere to be found. However, Bugs kept popping up everywhere – including the kitchen.

"Listen, Doc," Bugs said. "Daffy went to Vegas with DJ."

Bugs led Kate to the garage. The spy car looked fast even when it was standing still. A minute later, Kate had strapped on her seat belt. Bugs Bunny had strapped on twenty. And the car sped out of the garage so fast the wheels didn't touch the ground!

In Las Vegas, DJ and Daffy pulled up in
front of a casino called the Wooden Nickel.
The front of the building was a giant image
of Yosemite Sam. The neon sign in front
read: "Now appearing: Dusty Tails."

Inside, DJ searched for Dusty Tails.
The lights went down, and music blared.
A pretty cowgirl appeared onstage,
surrounded by a dozen miniature
Yosemite Sams. It was Dusty.

Thinking fast, DJ grabbed one of
the little Sams and stole his costume.
Then he sauntered onto the stage.
When he got to Dusty, DJ spun her into
a strong embrace. "I'm DJ Drake, Damian's
son. I need to talk to you."

"My dad is missing," DJ told Dusty later, in her dressing room. "He told me to ask you about the Blue Monkey."

Dusty smiled sadly. "I'm so sorry, but I'm afraid that's what comes with being a spy."

"Aha!" Daffy said gleefully as DJ's eyes went wide. DJ's dad *was* a spy!

Dusty grabbed a playing card stuck to the side of her makeup mirror. "I was supposed to give your father this," she said.

"That's a stupid playing card," Daffy complained. "Not a diamond!" Disgusted, he waddled over to the door and threw it open . . .

. . . and found himself face-to-face with the real Yosemite Sam and his gang. And they were standing next to a lit cannon!

Boom! The cannonball blasted, hitting Daffy in the stomach. He flew through Dusty's mirror and the wall behind it, across the dance stage, and into a glass cabinet. Glass flew everywhere as Daffy was hurled into a fire extinguisher, which exploded into a mass of white foam.

DJ grabbed the card from Dusty just as Yosemite Sam stepped through the door. Following Daffy's path, he made his escape. A minute later, he thrust a hand into a mountain of foam and pulled out Daffy Duck.

"Despicable," Daffy said.

DJ and Daffy quickly climbed a ladder to a second-floor railing. One of Sam's gang grabbed DJ, and the playing card in his pocket fell out and drifted to the casino floor below.

DJ jumped for a chandelier. This was his big chance to use his stuntman moves. But he missed. A second later, he fell through a poker table and landed with a thud.

Out of the corner of his eye DJ saw the playing card fall into an electric card shuffler. It was shuffled along with several other cards and passed to a blackjack table. DJ hustled over to the table. Yosemite Sam sat across from him.

"Gentlemen, place your bets," said the dealer. It was Foghorn Leghorn.

Foghorn dealt DJ and Sam their cards. DJ eyed the stack Foghorn was holding. Dusty's card was halfway down the pile.

"Hit *me*," DJ said. Foghorn gave him a card. "Hit me again."

"Hit me!" Sam said.

"Wait your turn," Foghorn said.

"Hit me. Hit me. Hit me," DJ said.

"No! Hit *me*, frazznabbit!" Sam cried. His face was turning purple.

"I'll hit you when I hit you," Foghorn replied.

"Hit me. Hit me. Hit me," DJ said again.

Foghorn gave him three more cards . . . and the last one was DJ's card, the queen of diamonds.

DJ grabbed the card and took off. Sam stood up to follow, but then paused to peek at his card. "Hit me," he said.

Foghorn Leghorn picked up Yosemite Sam and whacked him on the bottom.

Seconds later, DJ and Daffy were back in the Gremlin. But when DJ turned the key, the car fell to pieces! Scrambling out of the car, DJ and Daffy raced down the street.

Boom! Boom! Boom! Cannonballs and bullets flew over DJ's and Daffy's heads. Sam and his gang were after them!

In the spy car, Kate and Bugs Bunny were cruising the streets of Las Vegas. "We're never going to find that duck!" Kate said, frustrated.

Bugs pointed up ahead. Daffy was in the middle of the street, waving his arms and screaming. DJ wasn't far behind.

Crash! The car ran right into Daffy, smashing him up against the windshield like a bug.

"Daff never misses a cue," Bugs said admiringly.

Minutes later, DJ was behind the wheel of the spy car. It tore through the streets at breakneck speed, fishtailing into alleys and onto sidewalks. Yosemite Sam and his cronies were right behind them.

Beside DJ, Kate tried to stay calm. But only Bugs Bunny actually *was* calm. "Are we gonna stop before we hit that wall up ahead?" he asked casually.

Right in front of them was the back wall of the Wooden Nickel Casino!

Meanwhile, at the evil corporate headquarters, the Chairman was looking angry. "Obtaining the Blue Monkey will not be easy," he said. "We now have to deal with two people, a rabbit, and a duck. Unless, Mr. Drake, you would like to save us the trouble of going after your son?"

Damian Drake, DJ's father, was hanging in a cage nearby. Mr. Chairman's evil henchmen had kidnapped him and locked him up. He scowled at the Chairman. "My son is going to kick your butt!" he shouted.

Back in the spy car, Daffy was cowering next to Bugs. "Oh, mother," he whispered.

Suddenly the dashboard flickered to life. "Taking you to Mother," a computerized voice said.

"Who's Mother?" Kate screamed.

No one answered. There was a giant roar, and flames shot out of the back of the car. Then it lifted off the ground and flew right over the casino!

The spy car didn't fly for long. When DJ flicked the turn signal, it careened downward . . . heading right toward the rocky Nevada desert!

DJ, Kate, and Daffy were all squished against the windshield. They groaned in misery.

Bugs appeared behind them, looking perfectly normal. "My ears popped," he said. "Anyone else's ears pop?"

Fortunately, the car ran out of gas right before it crashed. It hovered a few feet above the ground. DJ, Kate, Daffy, and Bugs squirmed out.

The four friends walked across the desert. DJ held up to the sunlight the playing card Dusty Tails had given him.

"Wow! See that?" DJ exclaimed. He showed the card to Kate. "That's the 'Mona Lisa.'"

Kate peered at the card. "The 'Mona Lisa' is in Paris," Kate said. "How are you going to get to France?"

"I don't know, but I'll do it somehow. I've got to save my dad!" DJ declared.

Daffy grabbed the card from him. "Whatever! I'm going to get that diamond."

"Not so fast! Get back here with my card!" DJ yelled.

"Hold it right there, duckface! You're not going anywhere without MOI!" Kate shouted at the same time.

"Or moi," Bugs said, grinning. He snapped his fingers, and instantly they were in Paris!

DJ, Kate, Bugs, and Daffy found themselves outside a gift shop in the Louvre, the famous museum that housed the "Mona Lisa." And, as if by magic, they were all dressed in ultrastylish clothes.

Kate looked down at her outfit. "We're in Paris!" she cried.

"I know it defies the law of physics, but I never studied law," Bugs said.

At that moment, Pepé Le Pew and his assistant emerged from behind the gift shop counter and approached DJ. Pepé's assistant handed DJ a stuffed Pepé toy. "To find ze Blue Monkey, you must view le 'Mona Lisa' through le playing card," the toy said in a mechanical voice. The real Pepé pulled DJ into the shop's dressing room and showed him an array of special spy gadgets – including a superpowered cell phone.

Upstairs in the gallery, DJ looked back and forth between the painting and the playing card in his hand. At first he didn't see anything. Then he noticed that the back of the card was kind of shiny. He pulled at a corner, and a clear sheet peeled right off!

"A window!" Bugs said.

DJ held the card up to the painting, and an old map of Africa appeared in front of the "Mona Lisa."

"Wow," DJ and Kate said together. Kate snapped a picture with her cell phone.

"I'll take that," said a voice behind them.

Everyone turned. Elmer Fudd was standing there. And he was holding a shotgun!

Bugs grabbed the card from DJ. He and Daffy went one way. DJ and Kate went another. Elmer took off after Bugs.

"I'm gonna blast that wabbit!" Elmer bellowed.

He chased Bugs into several paintings, across all kinds of landscapes. But he couldn't catch him. As usual, Bugs was too fast.

DJ and Kate paused to catch their breath. While DJ looked around for Bugs and Daffy, a huge hand grabbed Kate from behind.

"Kate!" DJ called. Mr. Chairman's henchman Mr. Smith was dragging her away!

DJ followed Mr. Smith and Kate to the Eiffel Tower, where a black helicopter was hovering. When he got to the top, Mr. Smith was pushing Kate up a ladder dangling from the copter. He held her phone/camera in his hand.

"Give me the girl!" DJ shouted over the roar of the copter's choppers.

Mr. Smith shrugged and grabbed on to the helicopter ladder. Then he dropped Kate right off the tower!

"Heeellllppp!" Kate screamed.

DJ leaped off the tower and pressed a button on his spy phone. A rescue line shot out and anchored itself to a section of the tower. A second later DJ swung down and grabbed Kate out of thin air.

Moments afterward, they landed in chairs at an outdoor café, right across from Daffy and Bugs!

"Okay, they've got the camera, which means they have the map," DJ said, getting down to business.

"We have the card, and the window. We can take another picture," Kate put in.

DJ got to his feet, a look of determination on his face. "Let's go!" he said.

A little while later, DJ, Kate, Daffy, and Bugs were trudging through the African jungle in search of the Blue Monkey. DJ hacked through the dense foliage with a machete as best he could, but it was slow going.

"This would've been a lot easier if we had traveled underground," Bugs said.

"Come on, it's only another six thousand feet in the thick, bushy direction!" DJ said cheerfully.

At that moment, there was a crashing sound from behind them.

"What was that?" Kate asked nervously.

A second later, a huge elephant thundered through the underbrush, carrying Granny, Tweety, and Sylvester!

Granny smiled down at everybody. "Would you like a lift?"

Before long, the elephant stepped into a giant plaza surrounded by stone monkeys. A long corridor at one end led to a stone monkey altar bathed in blue light.

"This is our stop," DJ said, sliding off the elephant's back.

"Enjoy the rest of your adventure," Granny called as she and the others rode away.

The friends approached the temple's altar. Daffy picked up a small toy monkey.

"This is the Blue Monkey?" Daffy said. He couldn't believe it. "I've been rooked! Shafted by the gods! I want my diamond. Where is my diamond? WHERE IS MY HUMONGOUS ROCK?" he shouted.

While he spoke, the altar sank into the ground. As it disappeared, a huge boulder suddenly fell from the sky, crushing Daffy. He had triggered a booby trap!

DJ quickly rescued Daffy from under the rock, and then they continued into the temple. The real Blue Monkey was right in front of them!

Daffy raced to the altar. "I'm rich!" he shrieked. "I'm affluent! My liquidity is assured!"

DJ laid a hand on Daffy's arm, pulling him back. "Hey, Daffy, no! Get back here!"

Daffy was just inches away from the diamond. "It's mine! So close! It's mine!" he cried.

DJ pushed past him. "Do you mind?" he said.

"Mind? I've been shot, squashed, punctured, and liquefied for this diamond. Why should I mind?" Daffy asked sarcastically.

DJ solemnly stepped forward and picked up the Blue Monkey. Inside, the face of a monkey looked back at him.

"This is for you, Dad," DJ said, holding the diamond aloft.

"How sweet," said a voice behind them. Granny! Only it wasn't Granny. It was the Chairman in disguise. "Mr. Devil! Mr. Smith!" he called.

Mr. Smith and the Tasmanian Devil appeared, brandishing ray guns. They shot them at DJ, Kate, Bugs, and Daffy. Instantly, our heroes disappeared . . . and then rematerialized moments later inside ACME headquarters.

"Now give me the diamond," the Chairman ordered DJ.

"Never!" DJ declared.

"I see you require encouragement," the Chairman sneered. He pointed a remote control at a big TV screen. On the screen was Damian Drake, tied to train tracks inside ACME's warehouse. An enormous locomotive was headed straight for him.

"Do the right thing, DJ!" Damian shrieked. "Forget about me! You have to protect the diamond!"

But DJ was determined to save his dad, no matter what the cost. He tossed Mr. Chairman the diamond. However, instead of setting DJ, Kate, Bugs, and Daffy free, Mr. Chairman set his henchmen on them!

"Hey! What about my dad?!" shouted DJ.

"He's waiting for a train," Mr. Chairman said smugly. "Send in Marv!" Instantly, Marvin The Martian appeared. Mr. Chairman handed him the Blue Monkey Diamond. "Now off into space with you."

Mr. Chairman turned to DJ and his friends. "Once he installs the diamond in the ACME satellite, it's the end of humanity as we know it. The satellite will shoot a beam that will change the entire human population into monkeys!"

"Not while I'm around!" shrieked Daffy. He squirmed away from the Chairman's henchmen and rushed after Marvin. Bugs followed at his usual casual pace.

Daffy and Bugs stole a flying saucer and blasted off into space after Marvin. They pulled up next to Marvin's saucer. Bugs motioned for him to roll down his window.

Marvin looked annoyed, but he did it. "What is it, annoying earthlings?" But before Bugs and Daffy could answer, Marvin was instantly sucked out his window into the vacuum of deep space.

Daffy turned to Bugs. "Whaddaya know, he fell for it. Guess I owe you five bucks."

Back at ACME headquarters, Mr. Chairman's henchmen had hurled DJ and Kate into the ACME warehouse. A huge, scary robo-dog was guarding them. Kate was terrified. But DJ had a plan. He grabbed a steel rod and circled the snarling animal. But when he tried to hit the robo-dog with it, the dog just gobbled up the pole in three bites.

"Be a good dog and let us by," DJ said.

"Maybe he wants to play fetch," Kate suggested nervously. She grabbed another metal pole and threw it. The dog caught it in his mouth, then ground it up into tiny pieces. When he spit them out, the pieces formed the words "BAD DOG."

"I'll distract him. You go save my dad!" DJ yelled. He pulled the dog by the collar, trying to get him to chase his own tail.

Kate ran toward Damian Drake. The robo-dog tried to stop her, but DJ was too quick for him. He snagged a hook to the dog's collar, and the dog swung up into the air. He crashed into the wall and exploded.

DJ rushed toward his dad, desperately trying to untie his knots. The train was getting closer and closer! Kate screamed and closed her eyes. Just when it looked like all hope was lost, DJ pulled his dad to safety!

Damian Drake looked at his son proudly. "Wait till I tell my friends at the Agency about you, son."

"Come on," DJ answered. "If we wait around here any longer, we'll all be monkeys."

Meanwhile, up in space, Bugs was floating toward Marvin's flying saucer to retrieve the Blue Monkey Diamond. But instead, he found himself face-to-face with a ray gun . . . held by an angry Marvin The Martian. He'd survived! Marvin blasted Bugs into a bubble that floated through space. Then he headed for the satellite with the diamond.

Watching from inside the saucer, Daffy knew it was up to him to get the diamond. "Duck Dodgers to the rescue!" he shouted.

Daffy shot toward the satellite. Marvin was right behind him. He aimed his ray gun at Daffy, and Daffy disintegrated into a pile of ashes. Only his bill was still intact. But that was enough! One of Daffy's arms reached up from the pile and tossed the bill through space like a boomerang. It landed right on top of the satellite beam projector. The beam was blocked! All except for Daffy's nostril holes, which shot a teensy, tinsy beam toward earth . . .

. . . and hit the Chairman! He turned into a monkey right before Kate's, DJ's, and Damian's eyes.

Bugs and Daffy climbed back into their spaceship. "You saved the day, Daffy," Bugs said.

Daffy grinned. "Go on, you can say it . . . I'm your hhh . . . you know, rhymes with 'zero.'"

"Don't push your luck," Bugs told him.

Later on, Bugs and Daffy rejoined Kate, DJ, and Damian back in the ACME warehouse.

"Nice work, Daffy," DJ cheered.

Bugs Bunny put his arm around Daffy. "From now on, you and I are going to be equals," he promised. "No more second banana for you."

Daffy grinned. "Thanks," he said. "I really –"

SMASH! A giant beam landed on Daffy, squashing him flat.

The Warner Brothers' studio lights went up. "That's a wrap!" Kate called.

A horde of assistants surrounded Bugs, leading him away. The rest of the crew cheered and began to break down the movie set. Another wacky Looney Tunes adventure had been shot!

"Uh, hello?" a squashed-sounding voice called. It was Daffy Duck. "Can somebody help me up?"

THE END!